MW01154205

Words by Ekaterina Petrova • Pictures by Miretta Toncheva

SAVE IT FOR A RAINY DAY

Copyright Petrova Creative 2015.

For Baba Rita

"SAVE IT FOR A RAINY DAY, WHEN THERE'S NOTHING ELSE TO DO."

That's what Aunt Pearl said when April unwrapped her aunt's birthday gift. It was a small orange notebook. April had just turned eight.

"It's Moleskine," said Aunt Pearl, "used by the Great Writers of Old."

As April flipped through the book, the possibilities for filling its pages danced before her eyes. Stories, songs, drawings—oh my! April was ready to go.

"Hang on," she said. "I have to wait for it to rain? But we're in a drought!"

Aunt Pearl winked. "That's because you haven't been doing the rain dance I taught you. Let's see if you still remember it."

April and her aunt held hands. They shimmied their shoulders back and forth, high and low. They hopped around and sang,

"LET IT POUR!

LET IT POUR!

LET IT POUR!"

The two hopped and spun and sang until they fell to the floor in laughter.

"Well!" said Aunt Pearl, dusting herself off as she stood. "So you remember the dance after all! Just do it every night before you go to sleep. The rain will fall soon enough, and when it does you can use your new notebook. Until then," she winked again, "you be a good girl. Now let's get back to your party!"

That night, April practiced the rain dance alone in the dark, this time whispering,

"LET IT POUR,

LET IT POUR,

LET IT POUR."

Afterwards, she peeked out her window. There was no sign of rain.

April couldn't fall asleep that night. There were too many ideas floating around in her head.

"I know Aunt Pearl said to wait for a rainy day," she thought. "But maybe I'll write on just one page."

She pulled her blanket up over her head. Into this tent April brought a headlamp, an apple, a pen, and her new Moleskine notebook.

She felt a tingling in her hands—perhaps the spirit of the Writers of Old—as she wrote her name inside its cover.

Underneath, she wrote, "Stories and secrets and plans."

Satisfied, April closed the notebook and drifted off.

She woke with her dreams still fresh on her mind.

Aunt Pearl once said, "Writing down your dreams helps you remember them," so April grabbed her pen and wrote down the strange and wonderful things she had seen while she slept.

April brought her notebook to school that day, just in case.

During recess, she sat on the soccer field and wrote a poem.

the second grade is great
we really learn a bunch
I love music
I love math
but mostly
I LOVE LUNCH

She spent the entire rest of the day at her desk planning what to write next.
Ideas kept forming and flowing and, before she knew it, the bell rang.

April hurried home so she could keep creating. She locked herself in her room until she finished her next project: writing a play.

It was an adventure story about a group of friends who accidentally discover the remains of an ancient civilization while camping.

That evening, April got the neighborhood kids to try out for acting parts. They practiced all week, and the play turned out to be a big hit with the parents. They even got a standing ovation!

BUT WHILE APRIL'S WRITING CAREER WAS TAKING OFF...

...THE DAYS DRAGGED ON IN DRYNESS.

For weeks, April did the rain dance nightly, yet not a drop fell from the sky.
And despite her best intentions to wait for rain as her aunt had told her to,
April couldn't help but write nonstop.

She wrote songs.
She wrote lists.
She wrote jokes and haikus.
She wrote stories about hidden rooms and magic spirits,
letters to her future self,
letters to her future grandkids.

April wrote and she wrote and she wrote.

Sometimes, April drew as well. She drew things she loved and, using the "dream-boarding" technique Aunt Pearl once taught her, she drew things she hoped to have someday.

THE NOTEBOOK WAS FILLING UP FAST.

The day before Thanksgiving, April began a list of things she was thankful for. One page, then two. Her list went on and on.

- my parents
- Aunt Pearl
- Great Writers of OLD
- the smell after RAIN
- Friends
- KITTENS
- popsicles

April listened to her favorite album while she wrote and, before she knew it...

...the music had ended and there wasn't a single blank page left. Not one!

Horrified, April did the rain dance until she couldn't keep her eyes open anymore. "Please, please, please! Let it pour! Let it pour! Let it pour!" April pleaded until she fell asleep.

THE NEXT MORNING, THANKSGIVING MORNING...

April woke up to the pitter-patter of rain on the roof. She looked out into the grey, wet backyard and couldn't believe her eyes.

THE RAIN DANCE WORKED! IT WAS MAGIC!

April could hear her aunt singing in the kitchen.

Though the Tofurky smelled delicious, April felt sick to her stomach.

She wasn't sure how she would tell Aunt Pearl that she had already used up her entire notebook before she was supposed to, before a single day of rain.

April went downstairs to show her aunt what she had done.

"Are you angry?" April asked, her eyes brimming with tears.

Aunt Pearl laughed. "I was hoping you'd like it," she said with a wink. "In fact, I have one in every color, saved just for you. I had a feeling you were a writer."

Right then and there, Aunt Pearl pulled out another Moleskine.

April opened up the blank notebook, stuck her nose in it, and took a giant whiff. A rush of energy came over her.

45201137R00020

Made in the USA
Lexington, KY
19 September 2015